Santa's REINDEER Games

by Samantha Berger
Illustrated by John Manders

Scholastic Inc.
New York Toronto London Auckland
Sydney Mexico City New Delhi Hong Kong

For Holly, but of course.
— S.B.

For Emily, the E girl.
— J.M.

ISBN 978-0-545-36866-7

Text copyright © 2011 by Samantha Berger
Illustrations copyright © 2011 by John Manders

12 11 10 9 8 7 6 5 4 3 2 1   11 12 13 14 15 16/0

Printed in the U.S.A.   40
First printing, December 2011

DRUMROLL please . . .

Good people of the North Pole . . .
gingerbread men and gingerbread women . . .
snow angels and snow men . . . naughty and nice . . .

Welcome to Santa's Reindeer Games: the one event that will knock your snowshoes off and make you fa-la-la-la-lose your mind!

The winners of the Reindeer Games get the highest of honors . . . they get to pull my sleigh on Christmas Eve, and bring presents to all the children of the world!

We begin with the classic Ornament on a Spoon Race! The first deer who makes it down Santa Claus Lane without dropping their ornament wins!

Let's get ready to **REINDEEEEEEEEER!**

The racers are off!

Dasher is in the lead, followed by Donner and Blitzen, but here come Melvin and Dunder.

But Melvin trips over a Yule log and **SMASH!** down goes the ornament.

Then Dunder doesn't see that poinsettia plant . . .

OOPH!

. . . and he crashes into a very long strand of lights.

Dasher leaps back into the lead and wins!
All is calm, all is bright for Dasher, here at the
Reindeer Games . . . and the crowd goes wild!

Next is Pin the Tail on the Polar Bear. Dancer, Prancer, Trumpy, and Fifi will be blindfolded and must pin this tail on that bear's bottom.

Let's get ready to **REINDEEEEEEEEEER!**

The blindfold seems to be throwing Trumpy off, and he pins the tail on an ice sculpture of Mrs. Claus!

CRASH!

Down goes Trumpy, down goes the ice sculpture, and down goes Fifi!

Dancer flies, Prancer skates! They meet at the bear
AND PIN THE TAILS!

This truly is the hap-happiest time of the year
for Dancer and Prancer . . . and the crowd goes wild!

The next Reindeer Game is the Stocking Hop!
Each Reindeer climbs into a giant stocking, and
races down Jingle Bell Square in the frosty air.

Let's get ready to **REINDEEEEEEEEER!**

Comet and Cupid are hopping straight and steady.

Laverne is dashing through the snow, but can she keep up that pace?

And Skidders is rolling his way toward the finish line! There is nothing in the rules about rolling.

But Skidders rolls right into a mistletoe tree!
And Laverne is hopping her heart out, but when it
comes to keeping up with Comet, there's very little
ho-ho-hope.

This really 'tis the season to be jolly with a win
like that for Comet . . . and the crowd goes wild.

In Bobbing for Candy Canes . . . the winner is Donner!

In the Icicle Obstacle Course . . . it's Cupid!

And in Santa Says . . . it's a tie between
Blitzen . . . and Laverne!

There they are, ladies and gentlemen, the winners of the Reindeer Games: Dasher, Dancer, Prancer, Vixen, Comet, Cupid, Donner, Blitzen . . . and Laverne.

They will be the true stars this Christmas as they —

Um, yes, anyway, these eight reindeer are your Reindeer Games Champions!

It's a beautiful sight, we're happy tonight, because thanks to these top-notch reindeer, all the good children will have presents on Christmas morning!

If there's one thing we know about this dream team
. . . they'll go down in history.

And the crowd goes wild.